BOMBER BOYS

Thomas Bloor

BBC
LARGE
PRINT

First published in 2008 by
Barrington Stoke Ltd
This Large Print edition published
2010 by BBC Audiobooks
by arrangement with
Barrington Stoke Ltd

ISBN 978 1 405 62292 9

British Library Cataloguing in Publication Data available

Printed and bound in Great Britain by
CPI Antony Rowe, Chippenham and Eastbourne

A Note from the Author

Towards the end of the Second World War many RAF crew were very young, often only 18 or 19. They could almost still have been at school. Until you looked into their eyes. Then you saw how the strain of flying in combat, night after night, always left its mark.

I want to thank Peter Bloor, my uncle, for his help. He told me a lot about his time on an RAF bomber station and also lent me the book *Lancaster at War* by Mick Garbett and Brian Goulding. *Bomber Crew* by James Taylor and Martin Davidson also gave me plenty of ideas.

Volunteers like Nelson, the West Indian bomb aimer in the book, came from all around the world to fight alongside the British in the Second World War—a fact to be remembered.

For my Uncle Pete

Contents

Chapter 1

The Old Man

Spring 1944

The Old Man was gone. He must have been five years older than the rest of us. At least 23. We called him Skipper, or Smithy, or Bill, as well as the Old Man. But in the air force, he was Flight Lieutenant William Smith, killed in action, January 12th 1944. He was a good pilot and a decent bloke. He got us home that night, safe and well. All except for himself, that is.

We were a team. We'd been through training together, learning to fly the big beast of a plane they call the Lancaster bomber. William Smith had been our pilot, the captain of the plane. I was navigator, plotting our way to the target and back again.

Nelson was the bomb aimer. He pressed the button that dropped our bombs. Hammers was the flight engineer. He took care of the engines and helped fly the plane. Mitch was our radio operator, Dodge manned the guns in the upper turret and Ron was the rear gunner, our own Tail-End Charlie. Seven of us. We'd lived together, flown together, gone on leave together. We did everything together.

But now the Old Man had gone. He'd pulled off a perfect landing in a field half a mile from the air base, after a leak in one of the tanks left us too short of fuel to get all the way home. But somehow he'd hit his head, hard, when the plane came lurching to a stop. He was dead before the ambulance arrived. So now we had to get a new pilot.

His name was Johnny King, and I didn't like him from the start.

'Well then, boys,' he said, the first time we met him. 'What happened to your old skipper, then?'

None of us wanted to talk about it. I looked away and said nothing. Hammers broke the silence.

'The Old Man copped it,' he said. 'He's gone west.' He meant 'dead' but no one used that word.

'So I heard,' said Johnny. 'Well, you know what they say—' He paused for a moment. 'If he can't take a joke he shouldn't have joined up!'

It sounds cruel but we all laughed. We tried not to be too serious in those days, most of all about death. The night Bill died had been our third bombing mission. Operations, they called them, ops for short, and you had to do 30 to complete a tour. Once you'd done 30 ops your tour was over and you could get moved to a nice safe job working at one of the training schools. But you had to get through your tour first. And though no one said so, it was pretty clear that very few blokes ever made it to

30 ops.

We were walking down a country lane with the birds singing in the trees and the early spring lambs bleating in the fields. We'd been due to fly the first mission with our new pilot that night, but the weather forecast had said there was going to be fog. There was no sign of fog now, but we weren't going to complain. Johnny had offered to buy us all a drink.

'The way I heard it,' Johnny said, 'was that your skipper stayed too long at the controls. That he made mistakes. Is that true?'

Mitch coughed. 'He was all right, was Bill. Couldn't have met a nicer bloke.'

Johnny shrugged. 'Fair enough. But you boys don't need to worry any more. I don't make mistakes. And to tell the truth, it doesn't matter even if I do. You see, I'm lucky. Just plain lucky.'

A hare loped across the lane in

front of us. The air was filled with the smell of fresh new grass. I hoped Johnny was right, and that his luck would rub off on the rest of us. It was hard to believe that only three days ago we'd been fighting for our lives, thousands of feet up in the skies above Germany. And in a day or two we'd be doing it all over again.

Chapter 2

The Horse Shoe

We used to meet in the Horse Shoe. It was a small pub. The bar wasn't much bigger than the front room of a medium-sized house, but it was close to our air base, RAF Lime Coldham. It was always packed with air force people. That night the pub seemed even fuller than usual.

May Miller was going out as we were coming in. I almost bumped into her. She smiled.

'Hello, you.' She put her hand on my sleeve, near the cuff of my air force tunic. She was a WAAF, the women's branch of the air force. Her uniform was the same grey-blue serge as my own.

'May.' I stood still.

'Come on, Len, we've not got all night.' Hammers grabbed me by the arm and marched me into the heat of the crowded bar. I looked back at May and saw her shake her head with a sad smile on her face. Her eyes were shining as if they were full of tears. She turned and headed for the door.

'Girl friend?' Johnny King's face was close to mine. I didn't like it.

'Not any more,' said Hammers. His mouth formed a firm, straight line. 'She's an ex girl friend, that one.'

'Really?' Johnny craned his neck to stare over at the door and watch as May walked out. 'What's the matter with her? She looks rather good, to me.'

'She's bad luck. Puts the hex on any bloke she goes out with.'

Johnny raised his eyebrows, a mocking smile on his face. 'Really?' he said again.

I winked at Nelson. His dark face grinned back. We all knew that Hammers was the one man in

Bomber Command who believed in the power of lucky charms and all that. Johnny was going to have to accept it if he wanted to be our new skipper. As for me, I didn't like the look on Johnny King's face when he watched May walk out of the pub.

'She's cursed, she is.' Hammers wagged his finger in the air.

Dodge rolled his eyes. 'Here we go again,' he said.

Hammers took no notice. 'The last three lads she went out with,' he went on, 'were all air crew here at Lime Coldham, and now all of them have gone for a burton.' That was another way of saying they were dead. Hammers knew more slang words for death than anyone else at the base. 'Barker, remember him? Bought it over Belgium. Our Stevie never came back from Hamburg. And that Canadian bloke, Jobson, he hit a hillside in thick fog, three miles from home. All of them goners. And what's more, their crews went with them. That's 21 men, all told. She's the kiss of death, that one, make no mistake.'

'Her name's May. You could at least call her by her name.' I didn't want to listen to Hammers blaming May for what happened to those planes. The way he went on, you'd think she'd jumped into a night fighter and shot them all out of the sky herself. I wanted to defend her. But a moment later I was sorry I'd said it.

'May, hmm? Pretty name.' Johnny licked his lips. 'I'll have to take her out some time.'

'Have you been listening to a single word I've said, skipper?' Hammers stared at Johnny.

Johnny smiled. 'Look, I told you. There's nothing to worry about. I'm a lucky charm. A curse like that can't touch me.'

'Well, we could all do with a bit of extra luck, eh, boys?' Nelson smiled and nodded and nudged Hammers in the ribs with a playful elbow. He was smoothing things over in his usual warm-hearted manner. 'But didn't you say something about drinks, skip?'

'Of course!' Johnny turned to me. He patted his pockets and pulled a face. 'I say, Len,' he said, in a soft voice. 'I don't suppose you could lend me a quid? I've left my wallet behind!'

I sighed and felt in my tunic pocket. I didn't like Johnny King, but Nelson and Hammers were already calling him 'skipper'.

It looked like the rest of the crew were willing to accept him. As for myself, I still wasn't sure.

Chapter 3

Taylor's Warning

That night we all smoked our names onto the ceiling of the Horse Shoe. Grasping a lit candle in one fist, we were lifted up, one at a time, onto the back of our tallest crewman, Nelson. And we reached up to let the candle flame lick against the white plaster. We left dark, soot-stained letters on the ceiling. Urged on by loud cheers, we wrote our names up there for every one to see.

We weren't the first. In fact, we'd found it hard to find a clear spot anywhere on that ceiling. There were hundreds of names up there. A few of them we knew. But most of them were the names of boys who had been and gone. Boys no one remembered.

Nelson bent his knees while

Hammers and Johnny, laughing, hauled me off his back. Ron took the candle, ready to make his mark. I wondered how many of those who'd written their names up there were still alive. It wasn't a happy thought. I made my way through the thick crowd of drinkers, to the door. I needed air. Behind me I heard the bell above the bar ring out and the landlady called, 'Time, gentlemen, please!'

*   *   *

Outside I ran into Taylor. He was on his own, as he always was. He was clutching half a pint of pale ale, leaning against the brick wall of the pub's outside toilet. I tried to walk past, but the moment he noticed I was there he stood up straight and came stumbling towards me. He stood there, swaying from side to side, squinting at me in the dim light that filtered through the smoked glass windows of the pub.

We all knew Taylor, though none of us ever spoke to him. He'd been part of a bomber crew himself, once. Not any more. It was said he'd broken down in tears one night and refused to fly on any more ops. The air force labelled him L.M.F. This stood for Lack of Moral <u>Fibre</u>. It meant that he was branded as a coward. He'd been reduced to the lowest of ranks and moved out of his squadron. They sent him here, to Lime Coldham. He got all the worst jobs on the base, like cleaning out the toilets in the heat of the summer, or digging out drainage ditches in the middle of winter, when the ground was frozen solid. And no one ever talked to him. Not a word.

I don't know about the others, but I know why I avoided Taylor. It wasn't because I looked down on him as a coward or thought he was a disgrace to king and country or anything like that. It was because I was afraid. I was afraid I could easily end up just like him. Seeing Taylor made me remember how scared I was, when I had to go on ops. So I kept away from him. But now here we were, face to face.

Most of the time Taylor didn't even try to talk to anyone. But tonight it was plain he'd had a lot to drink. He looked at me and shook his head.

'Don't fly with Lucky Johnny King,' he said. His voice was thick with drink.

'What?' I looked hard at him. 'What did you say?'

'Lucky Johnny King,' he said again. 'He was with my old squadron. Whatever you do, don't fly with him. He may well be lucky, but nobody that flies with him ever is. Ask him. His last two planes both went down in flames. And the crews, all of them were killed. All except him. So don't fly with Johnny King. Not if you want to live!'

This was not what I wanted to hear.

'Shut your mouth!' I pushed Taylor away. He staggered back and sat down hard at the side of the road. His beer slopped out of the glass and spilled all over him. He sat there blinking, as if he hadn't noticed what I'd done.

'Don't fly with Johnny King,' he said again.

Chapter 4

Jump

I turned away, my heart pounding and my cheeks burning with shame. Taylor wasn't so bad. He'd had a tough time, that was all. It wasn't right to go pushing him around like that. I shouldn't have done it. I took a couple of deep breaths and then I looked back. I meant to go over and help him up, but he was already gone. He must have staggered away somewhere while I wasn't looking.

The pub door swung open and a babble of happy voices flooded out into the night air. The rest of my crew came to join me.

Nelson had his arm around Johnny King's shoulder. 'I've just asked our new captain to bring his few bits and pieces into our wonderful Nissen hut,' he said with a grin. The Nissen hut was like a large shed, built on the edge of the air field. It was where the seven of us lived, all together, as most bomber crews did. The Old Man's bunk had been left empty, until now.

'It's an honour to become part of the family,' Johnny said. He looked around, grinning at us all. 'Now, who's for a spot of midnight madness?'

*   *   *

The old stone bridge crossed the stream on the way back to RAF Lime Coldham. We cut across some farm land to get there. Johnny ran ahead with Dodge and Hammers. We could hear them whooping and shrieking as they skidded on the slippery mud. Ron and Mitch were a little way ahead of us.

'You children go ahead and have some fun!' Nelson called. He laughed in his deep and easy way. I fell into step beside him.

'Nelson. What do you make of the new skipper?'

Nelson's eyebrows shot up. 'He's all right. I think he'll fit in. He's almost one of us already, don't you think? Why do you ask?'

'Oh, nothing,' I said. I laughed. But I was uneasy.

'Look, don't take any notice of what he said about May,' Nelson said. 'He wasn't being serious. And if you want to know what I think, if you really like the girl you should see her. Don't listen to Hammers. He's like a brother to me, you all are, but even I can see the man's a bit of an idiot!'

I fell silent. What Nelson said made perfect sense. It was nonsense to think that you could control luck. Sometimes things just happened. And I did want to see May again. More than anything. So I couldn't bring up what Taylor had said about Johnny King. Lucky or unlucky, blessed or cursed, the truth was that our lives depended on how well we did our different jobs when we flew *M for Mother*. And, of course, on how well our enemies did theirs, when they tried to shoot us down.

It didn't matter who sat at the controls of your plane, or which girl you chose to go out with, or how many lucky charms you carried in your pocket. None of that made any difference. It couldn't affect the aim of the German flak gunners, firing up through the clouds. It couldn't affect the search-lights that probed the sky with their great fingers of burning light, or the night fighter pilots, watching and waiting in the darkness. So I said nothing. I tried to forget about Taylor and what he'd said about Lucky Johnny King.

When we got to the bridge Johnny was standing on the low stone wall.

'At last we're all here!' he said. 'And now, for no reason at all, one of us is going to jump into the stream!'

19

A ragged cheer greeted these words.

'I'm glad you approve. Who'd like to go first?'

We all laughed. But Johnny was serious. He pointed at me.

'You! Len. Pilot Officer Poll. Over the side of the bridge with you!'

I took a step back. 'Come off it, Johnny, that stream's only a few inches deep. I'll break my legs.'

'Come off it, *sir*, I'll break my legs, *sir*, don't you mean? I outrank you, Len, remember?'

Of course that was true. Johnny was a flight lieutenant and therefore he was my superior officer. But within the close team spirit of a bomber crew no one had ever taken much notice of that. Until now.

'Well? I'm waiting. I want you to jump. Do I have to make it an order?'

The rest of the boys were still laughing, but now they sounded a little bit strained. A silence fell.

20

Johnny King was staring at me. I looked right back at him. I didn't move. Then a voice from behind us broke the silence.

'Where the devil have you lot been? I've been riding round these blasted country lanes for hours looking for you!' It was Trevor Price-Jones, the intelligence officer from the bomber station. He was sitting astride his bike and glaring at us. He was furious. 'The fog's gone. The op's back on. We go tomorrow!'

Chapter 5

Before We Flew

May. I had to see her before we flew out on the raid. Lying on my bunk in the Nissen hut, with Nelson's gentle snoring filling the fusty air, I could think of nothing but May. May and the raid.

It was going to be Berlin. Somehow I knew it. Berlin was one of the best-defended targets. And it was also deep into Germany and a long way to go. A flight to Berlin and back could take as much as ten hours. That was, if you made it back at all.

After breakfast I went straight up to the flight office to make sure Price-Jones hadn't been playing a cruel joke on us the night before. But no. My name was up on the notice board under *M for Mother*, along with the rest of the crew. For the first time, I saw the name 'Flight Lieutenant Johnny King' written in white chalk where it said 'Pilot'.

I cycled out onto the air field to start the day's work. There was a lot to do before a raid. All morning I would be busy checking and re-checking the navigation gear aboard our Lancaster, *M for Mother*.

There she was, standing on the tarmac, looming through the morning mist like a giant pre-historic bird, stretching her wings at the dawn of time. The four huge propellers were all still, as if frozen in the chilly air. The Perspex bubble in the bomber's nose was pointing towards the horizon. This was where Nelson would lie at full length and watch for the right moment to press the bomb release button and send our deadly load on its way down. My navigator's table, with its charts and instruments, was hidden away inside, at the back of the cockpit.

The ground crew were climbing all over our aeroplane. Half a dozen lads in overalls and wellies were working away on *M for Mother*, making sure everything was in order for tonight.

I took a deep gulp of the cold morning air and fought down the sick feeling in my belly. The bombers were being loaded with plenty of fuel. That meant a long trip. Berlin, I was sure of it! I tried to put the thought out of my mind. There wasn't time to sit around brooding. Not if I wanted to see May before the op.

After I'd finished a proper check of my section of the aircraft, I hurried over to the operations block where May worked. I knew her shift was starting soon. The WAAFs spent their nights in a block one or two miles away. They were transported in by lorry every morning.

I was early. May hadn't arrived yet. I waited by the office entrance.

A cold wind swept over the air field, plucking at the collar of my tunic. Suddenly Trevor Price-Jones was at my elbow.

'Shouldn't you be somewhere else? Aren't you on ops tonight? For God's sake, man, go and get some kip!'

He meant I needed to sleep, and he was right. I nodded and walked away, moving around the building until I was out of his sight. I couldn't face an argument with Price-Jones. My guts were already turning over at the thought of the raid that night. Behind the accounts block, I leant against the wall and waited, my hands stuffed into my tunic pockets and my back hunched against the cold. The spring sunshine of the day before seemed to have gone for good.

At last, I heard the roar of a motor and saw the truck arrive. It came to a stop outside the office block. The tail-board dropped and a group of WAAFs climbed out. There was May, easy to spot with her blonde hair swept back and tied in a head-scarf.

I took my hands out of my pockets and was about to wave when suddenly my arms were grabbed and pinned to my sides. A voice in my ear said, 'Oh, no, you don't! I'm not having a curse put on *M for Mother* just because you can't leave May Miller alone!'

It was Hammers. He dragged me back behind the accounts building and by the time I'd struggled out of his grasp, May and the others had vanished into the offices. And Trevor Price-Jones was standing in the doorway again, hands on his hips, staring at me. There was nothing more I could do. I knew I wouldn't be able to see May again before tonight. And by then it could be too late.

Chapter 6

Hammers' Luck

'It's for your own good, Len! You'll thank me later!' Hammers called after me. I didn't look back as I stalked away.

I went back to the Nissen hut and lay on my bunk. Nelson was still asleep. Nothing ever seemed to worry Nelson, not even the thought of an air raid on Berlin. There was a tight feeling in my chest and I was finding it hard to breathe. I was angry. Really angry.

When Hammers came into the hut I had to stop myself from jumping up and hitting him. I lay there and gritted my teeth instead. I listened to him rummaging among his belongings.

It wouldn't be long before we had to head over to the briefing room, to

27

be told our target for tonight. Then it would be off to the mess for bacon and eggs. Then the lorry would pick us up, take us to the parachute station to pick up our 'chute and our flying kit, then on to our waiting Lancaster. I found myself wishing we were already on our way.

Hammers was still rooting around over by his bunk. He was really getting on my nerves.

'Right,' said Hammers, standing up and looking at me. 'A joke's a joke, but this is going too far!' There was a catch in his voice. I was amazed to see he was shaking. 'Len, if you've taken it, I swear I'll—'

'Taken what?' I said.

'Don't pretend you don't know! Just give it back and we'll say no more about it.'

I sat up on my bunk. 'I don't know what you're talking about.'

Now it was Hammers who looked as if he wanted to hit me. He clenched both his fists.

'My lucky bottle top. Give it back!'

I almost laughed in his face. But then I saw how pale he was. Hammers was terrified. He really believed an old bottle top would help bring him safely home from the raid. And he couldn't find it.

'I haven't got your bottle top,' I said.

'You must have!' Hammers stared at me. His face was scarlet. 'You were angry with me about May Miller. So you took it. Now give it back. Please!'

There was a tense silence. Hammers sat down on the nearest bunk. He buried his face in his hands.

I stood up. I wasn't angry any more. I now felt as scared as Hammers. We were a team. We had to stay together. I couldn't let Hammers break down like this.

'Come on,' I said. 'I'll help you look for it.' I went over to Nelson's bunk and shook him by the shoulder. 'Can you give us a hand, Nelson?'

Johnny King breezed into the hut a few moments later, to see us all on our hands and knees peering under the bunks and into every corner of the dimly lit hut.

'What's going on?' he said.

'Hunt the thimble, skipper,' said Nelson. 'It's what this crew always does. We find it a fun way to pass the time before an op.'

Johnny shrugged. 'Time we were off to the briefing room.'

We never did find Hammers' lucky bottle top.

Chapter 7

Target for Tonight

It was getting dark outside as we trooped into the briefing room. We were all there. Nelson and poor old Hammers, who looked sick with nerves. Johnny King, Dodge, Ron and Mitch and all the other bomber crews from the squadron. As always, the intelligence staff had pulled a large curtain across the front wall, covering up the huge map that would tell us all we needed to know about the mission.

A hush fell. We waited. Trevor Price-Jones stepped up and tugged on a little cord. The curtain rolled back and there it was. The name of our target, as large as life. And I'd known it all along. Berlin.

A chorus of low groans filled the room when everyone saw where we were going. Trevor Price-Jones looked up, angry, his moustache twitching. But it was all right for him. He didn't have to fly to Berlin.

'Don't worry, boys,' Johnny said. 'It'll be a piece of cake!'

'Not exactly lucky, though, is it?' I said. 'First op with you as skipper and we get Berlin!'

Johnny looked at me. He was smiling but his eyes were cold. 'You can always ask to switch to a different crew, Len.'

But I couldn't leave the others. I'd never flown with anyone else. And Johnny King knew it. I shook my head and hoped I wouldn't regret my decision.

Chapter 8

Safety in Numbers

Maps. Co-ordinates. Calculations. Figures. Numbers. That's all I thought about when we were in the air. I sat at my cramped navigator's station, with the canvas curtain drawn closed, cutting me off from everyone and everything except my maps, the calculations I was making and my numbers.

I didn't think about what might be happening in the rest of the plane, or about all the other bombers flying alongside us, or about the German night fighters, the anti-aircraft guns and the search-lights. I didn't think about the bombs in our bomb bay, those huge metal canisters, as big as a man, packed full of explosives. I didn't think about where they fell or who they might hit when they reached the ground. All I thought about was how to work out where we had to go and how we'd get back home again. And to do that, I had my numbers.

There was a bad feeling about this op. I think we all felt it, though no one wanted to say so. So it was more important than ever that I should concentrate on plotting our course. There were so many things that could go wrong. Things that were out of my hands. But there was this one task I knew I could do, and do well. I could navigate. I could guide this aeroplane to Berlin and back.

I had my leather flying helmet on, with its built-in ear-phones. I heard a crackle of static and then Johnny King's voice sounded in my ears.

'Where are we now, Len?'

My oxygen mask was attached to the helmet, but I'd left it hanging by one strap. There was a mike fitted in the mask so I could talk to the pilot and the rest of the crew over the intercom. We weren't up high enough yet to need the oxygen, and the mask gave me sores on my face if I wore it for too long. But now I needed to speak to the skipper, so I lifted the mask up to my mouth.

'Checking the course now, skipper. Five minutes to the coast. And we're about a mile too far to port. Can you double check that on the roller map, Nelson?'

As well as being bomb-aimer, Nelson also served as back-up navigator, though his equipment was a lot simpler than mine. He just had the roller map, which was like a roll of toilet paper, printed with a chart that followed our intended course.

'Right ho,' Nelson's voice came back. There was a pause and then he spoke again. 'I can see the river. And there's the railway. So, yes, that makes us just over a mile to port.'

I was busily jotting down some quick calculations. Then I lifted the mask to my face again. 'Change course, three degrees.'

'Three degrees. OK.'

Next I had to calculate our ground speed using the G-Box, one of the latest gadgets we had to help us navigate. When I knew our speed I could then work out just how long it would take us to arrive at our target. I would always calculate it right down to the last second. Of course, I was never one hundred per cent right, but I liked to see how close I could get.

Now Nelson's voice crackled into my ear. 'Here's the coast, coming up, just like you said it would, Len.'

'Does that surprise you?' I said.

'Not for a moment.'

Even over the crackly intercom I could hear the smile in his voice. And suddenly I felt good. Everything was going to be all right. We were the best bomber crew on the base, even if the Old Man had gone. This was just another mission. We'd done this three times already, why not a fourth? Why not 30? I'd find our way to the target, Nelson would drop our bombs and then I'd find our way home. What could go wrong?

Chapter 9

Thousands of Feet Beneath Us

We headed out across the North Sea. I knew the sea was down there, thousands of feet beneath us, deep and cold and dark. But I tried not to think about it.

The G-Box had given us a good start, but I wouldn't be able to use it once we got over enemy territory. It didn't work well at long range, and besides, the Germans had figured out a way of jamming the signal. Beyond the North Sea, the G-Box was useless.

I needed to have my wits about me when we reached the enemy coast. So now was the time for what always hit me this stage of the op. Air sickness. Well that's what I called it. Every time we flew on an op I had to throw up. There was a chemical

38

toilet towards the rear of the plane. I made my way there, clambering over the main spar first, and then the rear spar, banging my head on the raw iron-work more than once on my way.

I passed Dodge, seated in front of his radio transmitter. He'd taken off his flying jacket and was just in shirt-sleeves. The radio operator hardly ever got cold in a Lancaster—his station was right next to the heating vents. Dodge gave me the thumbs up as I crawled past. He once told me he wouldn't have felt right flying on an op if I didn't get sick. I wasn't going to let him down.

As I struggled over the spar again and back to my desk, I looked up and saw the cockpit, drenched in silver moon-light. There was Johnny at the controls, flying with his left hand on the control stick and his right resting on his knee. Hammers sat beside him, his eyes flickering over a panel of instruments. The glowing dials shed a feeble orange light onto his rigid face. Two shiny metal fire extinguishers glimmered in their fittings on the panel above his head.

Back behind my curtain I sat scribbling away on my notepad. I was back among the numbers and all was fine. Then Johnny's voice broke the calm.

'Enemy coast just ahead of us, boys. The Germans have got a lot of flak around here. We could be in for a bumpy ride.'

Chapter 10

Cork-screw

I put my hand on my pencil and notepad to stop them sliding off the desk. We were climbing, higher and higher. Johnny was taking us up, hoping to keep out of range of the anti-aircraft guns. We needed our oxygen masks now. We'd all have passed out without them.

'Lots of fire-works.' Nelson was reporting the shell-fire he could see bursting beneath us. 'Nothing close to a hit, Skip. We're too high.'

'Just the way I like it.'

The engines droned. The time ticked by. I passed on more course calculations to Johnny King. We moved closer and closer to our target. And further and further away from home.

We'd been in the air for nearly

four hours when we had our first alarm. It came without warning.

'Enemy plane to port!' Mitch's voice, tight with fear, broke over the intercom. 'It's about a mile behind us. Damn! Lost it. It's gone into a bank of cloud.'

'See anything, Ron?'

'Not a thing.'

There was a tense silence, then suddenly Ron was shouting. 'Cork-screw right, skipper! Cork-screw right!'

I braced myself as I felt the plane lurch into a rolling dive. The cork-screw was the best way of shaking off an enemy fighter, but it wasn't much fun for the crew. The pilot threw the control column as far to the side as it would go and we spiralled down through the air, plunging thousands of feet, desperate to shake the fighter off our tail.

Then suddenly we were level again, flying as if nothing had happened. There was a minute or two of tense silence over the intercom. I sat at my desk. I hardly dared to breathe. I was waiting for the scream of bullets ripping through *M for Mother*.

At last Ron said, 'I think we lost him.'

I'd been gripping the desk so hard I found it difficult to let go. My fingers were sore and there was blood in my mouth where I'd bitten my lip.

'How far to the target, Len?' Johnny King sounded very offhand. Too offhand. We could have all been killed.

'Navigator?'

I took a deep breath and looked at the calculations I'd been working on before Mitch raised the alarm. I looked at my watch. I quickly worked out a new set of figures.

'We'll be there in 52 minutes, 35 seconds,' I said.

Chapter 11

Above the Inferno

I was wrong. It only took 51 minutes. Then we were over Berlin and things got very hot indeed.

'Target ahead.'

The flak was coming thick and fast and the search-light crews down on the ground were busy trying to trap us in their powerful beams. We called it getting coned. If they could see you, more and more search-lights would home in. Soon your Lancaster would be lit up like a Christmas tree and the flak gunners would shoot you out of the sky. If we wanted to get home again we had to stay hidden in the darkness until we could drop our bombs and make our escape.

'Aren't we a bit low, skipper?' It was odd how distant Hammers sounded over the intercom.

'We're fine.' Johnny King was so sure of himself. Maybe he really was some kind of lucky charm in human form. Maybe nothing could hurt us with Johnny at the controls.

'Bomb doors open.'

Now Nelson was guiding us in on our bombing run.

'Left. Left. Right. Steady. Steady.'

We had to fly straight and level so we could be sure of getting our bombs at least somewhere near our target, which was a factory district far below us. This was the most dangerous part of the operation. We were now easy to hit.

All around us the other bombers were closing in on the target, dropping their bombs, and then heading for home.

I bit my lip. I switched off my mike. 'Come on, Nelson!' I whispered under my breath. 'Drop the bombs! Drop the bombs and then we can get out of here!'

At last it came, Nelson's shout of 'Bombs gone!' I felt *M for Mother* jolt and lift as we suddenly found ourselves several thousand pounds lighter.

And then it happened. There was a terrible rending sound. The Lancaster lurched and tipped. The curtain between my navigator's station and the rest of the plane was suddenly ripped away.

'Christ!' someone said over the intercom. 'The port wing's been hit!'

'I said we were too low!' This was Hammers. 'Someone's dropped a bomb on us!'

The worst had happened. One of our own planes, another bomber crew like us, but flying somewhere up above, had dropped their bombs right on top of *M for Mother*. And now, to make matters worse, we'd been trapped in the beams of a search-light. There was nowhere to hide. The bomber was lit up, inside and out. I closed my eyes against the blinding glare.

'We've been coned!'

We were falling through the night sky, twisting and turning, trying to escape the light. But with so much damage to the wing, *M for Mother* could hardly hold a straight course, let alone escape the search-lights. I heard the crackle of anti-aircraft fire and then felt a terrible shuddering as the shells ripped into our Lancaster.

Suddenly the blazing lights went out. I was no longer blinded. The search-lights had lost us. I gaped. I looked out through the Perspex of the cockpit at the scene around us. I'd never wanted to take a look out beyond my curtain before. I'd always been happy to stay cooped up with my maps and my set square and slide rule. I'd never looked down at the target, or even out at the stream of bombers flying with us. But tonight was different. I had no choice. I looked.

It was a staggering sight. The sky

was lit with gunfire. Explosions burst in the air all around us. Planes lit up as search-lights hit them, or anti-aircraft shells set them ablaze. They peeled away, trailing smoke and fire. On the ground, fires burned a wild orange and flickering red. I could see a mass of green marker flares. These had been dropped by our path-finder squadrons, to help guide us to the target. Everywhere, as far as the eye could see, fires raged out of control. The city had been flooded by a sea of flame. How could anyone still be living in that inferno?

I stood up and stepped away from my desk. Great holes had been torn through the fuselage all along the length of the plane.

'Nelson? Ron? Anyone?' There was no reply. I pulled off my flying helmet and oxygen mask. In the cockpit, someone was wrestling with the control column. I could see it was taking every bit of his strength just to keep the plane level. And we were still falling. He lifted his head and I saw it was Hammers.

'Get out!' he shouted. 'For God's sake, go! I'll hold her as long as I can, then I'll follow you down.'

'What about the others? Where's Johnny?'

'Gone.'

I looked around. I thought I'd see him on the floor, either wounded or dead. He wasn't there. But I could see someone, down in the nose of the plane. Nelson. He was lying face down. He wasn't moving. I saw the dark glint of blood and looked away.

'Len!' Hammers yelled at me again. 'You have to bale out! You have to go now!'

I nodded, stupidly, and turned to get my parachute.

Chapter 12

City of Fire

I was numb with shock. I kept saying to myself, over and over again, 'This isn't happening. This isn't happening.' But it was. It was all too real. I picked up my parachute. My hands were shaking so much I could barely clip the straps onto my harness.

I looked back at Hammers. He was hanging onto the control column, desperate to keep *M for Mother* level so I could get out. His face was creased up with the effort, his tongue poking out of the corner of his mouth. I turned away and climbed down into the nose section, where the escape hatch was. That was the last I ever saw of Hammers.

The nose section had been badly shot up. Wind moaned through jagged holes in the Perspex. I tried not to look at Nelson, lying twisted amongst his wrecked bomb-aiming instruments. My best friend was dead.

The hatch was already open. And someone else was there, crouching beside the opening. It was Johnny King. He grabbed me by the arm and shouted into my face, bellowing to make himself heard above the whistle of the wind.

'My parachute's all shot up. We'll have to go together.' He grabbed hold of the straps of my chute and wrapped them around his wrists. 'Now jump!'

I didn't move. 'Are the others all right? Did you order the rest of the crew to bale out?'

Ron and Dodge had their own escape hatches to the rear of the plane. Mitch might have got out already. Nelson wasn't going anywhere. But I couldn't understand why Johnny was here, about to bale out, and not back at the controls, flying the plane with Hammers.

'Just jump!' Johnny yelled. 'Now!'

Still I waited, frozen with fear. I was confused and uncertain. Then Johnny King kicked at my shins and shoved me back. I tripped and, with Johnny still clinging to my parachute straps, we fell through the hatch and out into the night sky.

I'll never know whether it was Johnny King or me who pulled the D-ring to open the parachute. I have no memory of those first few moments of free-fall. The next thing I knew we were hanging in the air with the wind rustling through the straps and the silk 'chute rippling above. Johnny King was clinging onto me, his breath hot on my face.

I turned my head and saw *M for Mother* pass over us, heading down. She was lit up from inside by an orange glow of flame. That meant the end. The petrol tanks must have been hit. As I watched, the flames grew brighter, leaving a blazing stream of fire in the sky, and then the plane suddenly vanished. I looked away. Had any of the others got out, or were Johnny and I the only survivors?

The thought of survival made me look down. I wished I hadn't. We were heading for the ground faster than we should have been. Our parachutes were designed for one, not two. And we were falling into the jaws of hell.

The streaking lights of tracer bullets ripped through the darkness of the sky. The air was alive with burning flakes of fire, like tiny floating demons. Flares burst in showers of red, green and orange. And I could see the streets of the burning city spread out beneath us. The twisting roads were lit up by flames and bomb blasts. Whole rows of buildings seemed to vanish in sheets of leaping flame. This was what our bombs were doing. And I wasn't up in *M for Mother* any more, hiding behind my curtain with a head full of calculations. I was here, heading down fast towards the ruined streets, about to join the people we'd been tormenting, on the streets of their city of fire.

Chapter 13

Darkness and Light

Down we fell. A great pool of fire lay below us and we plunged towards it. The heat of the blazing buildings burnt my feet and legs. Smoke and ash swirled around us and a hot gust of wind filled our parachute and lifted us up and over the flames.

We came down in a patch of darkness beyond the blazing streets. Something tore at my flying jacket. One of my boots was ripped from my foot. The parachute snagged. Johnny gave a grunt of pain and then he was gone, dropping away from me. We'd landed in some trees, and the parachute had got caught in the branches, but I couldn't see a thing and I didn't know what to do.

'Are you going to stay dangling there all night?'

Johnny was standing just below me, his head level with my knees.

I unclipped my parachute harness and fell to the ground, hitting the earth with a jolt that took the breath out of me. I fell onto my side and lay there, gasping.

'Oh, get up, you big baby!'

Johnny had stripped off his leather jacket and his flying helmet. He was pacing up and down under the dark trees.

'Looks like we've come down in one of the city parks. But we can't go anywhere while the raid's still on. We should find somewhere to lie low for the rest of the night.'

I didn't say anything. I just staggered along behind him as Johnny made his way through the empty park, keeping to the cover of the trees and bushes.

'Look. That's a gardener's shed over there.'

A low wooden hut stood under a row of pine trees. Johnny kicked the door in. I noticed he still had both his boots on. I limped into the hut behind him and he pulled the door closed. Inside was complete darkness.

There was a smell of damp and earth. But the smoke of the burning city had got into the hut, too. It snagged in my throat every time I took a breath.

'Johnny.'

'What?' A voice in the dark.

'You lied.' I spoke softly. 'You said you were lucky. Why didn't you tell us about the others? The crews you'd flown with before? Dead, all of them.'

Johnny King gave a sniff. 'I said I was lucky, not my old crews. Can I help it if my luck didn't help them? I was hoping you lot would be different.'

'You left Hammers to die! You just baled out, soon as you could, and left him to keep the plane in the air! He never had a chance!'

'I'm a survivor,' said Johnny. 'This is war, not some silly game. Some of you boys need to grow up.'

'No chance of that happening to Hammers, is there? Or Nelson? Ron, Dodge and Mitch too, for all we know. None of them are going to grow up now, are they?'

'Keep your voice down, for God's sake! You'll alert every German for miles around!'

'What does it matter? They're going to catch us anyway. We're in the middle of Berlin! How are we going to get away?'

'Just shut up, will you? We'll think about that later. First, I need to get some rest.'

Outside, the shuddering rumble of the bombs and the pounding of the anti-aircraft guns went on and on. I closed my eyes in the darkness of the hut. But I knew there'd be no sleep for me that night.

*   *   *

The raid came to an end around four in the morning. Then it grew quieter for an hour or two. I watched the light of dawn seep into our hiding place. I heard the sound of birdsong.

It was morning, and Johnny King was peering out through a small, dusty window.

'I can see some people,' he said. 'A bunch of old women, it looks like. Didn't notice in the dark, but we're right on the edge of the park, next to a row of streets. This whole area has taken a terrible pounding. There's hardly a house left standing.'

'Johnny,' I said, 'do you think any of the others made it out of the plane?'

Johnny didn't reply. He went on looking at the scene outside.

'No sign of any soldiers or police. God, this place is a shambles!'

I gave a cough. The things I'd said a few hours ago were still racing around my head. I wasn't finished with Johnny King.

'Isn't it the pilot's job to keep the plane in the air while the crew bales out? You left Hammers at the controls. You didn't even give the order to bale out, did you? You just wanted to save yourself. That's all you were thinking about, from the moment we were hit.'

Johnny King turned and looked at me. I saw his eyes narrow.

'You left them too,' he said.

When I replied there was a catch in my voice. 'Do you think I don't know that?'

I could still see Nelson's body lying crumpled in the shattered nose of the Lancaster, and Hammers' face as he struggled with the control stick.

'Forget it.' Johnny turned back to the window. 'We're alive and they're dead. That's all there is to it.'

'Lucky Johnny King!' I gave a hollow laugh. Johnny took no notice.

'I'm going to talk to those old

women,' he said. 'I'll get them to give us something to eat. I don't know about you, but I'm starving!'

'You're going out? In your air force uniform? Don't you think the Germans out there might be a bit … angry?'

'After the pounding we've been giving them? Don't be daft! They'll be so scared they'll hand over all their grub the moment they see us. Come on.'

I shook my head. 'I'm staying here.'

'They're just old women, for goodness' sake!'

I didn't move.

Johnny gave a shrug. 'Please yourself. But I'm not coming back. You're on your own from now on. I can't have you tagging along if you're too scared to deal with a bunch of old ladies!'

He opened the door of the hut and left without looking back.

I watched from the window. It

looked like Johnny was right. People seemed to be scared of him. They were a ragged-looking crowd, dressed in tattered clothing. He went up to one frail old woman with frizzy silver hair. She was thin as a twig and looked as if she hadn't eaten in days. Towering over her, Johnny pretended to eat, rubbing his belly and shovelling spoonfuls of imaginary food into his mouth. When the woman just stared, Johnny raised his fist and shouted at her.

'Do as I say, you stupid crone!' he bellowed, although it was clear she couldn't understand him. Eyes wide, she shrank back in fear. Two other women, both as old and starved-looking as the first, quickly moved between Johnny and their friend. They smiled up at him, nodding and smacking their lips and patting their bellies. They led him away towards a street of bombed-out houses. The rest all shuffled after them and I lost sight of Johnny King in the crowd.

*   *   *

I was taken prisoner a few hours later. A German patrol made up of two elderly soldiers and a lad of around seventeen, a year or two younger than I was, kicked in the door to the little hut and pointed their guns at me.

I put my hands above my head and they marched me out of the park. We passed a row of houses with their front walls blown in, which gave way to great heaps of broken brick and rubble. Looking over this waste land I was shocked to see the body of a man dangling by his neck from the only lamp-post left standing in the street.

It was Johnny. They hadn't given him food. They'd hanged him.

One of the German soldiers shook his head. He looked grim. The young lad pointed at Johnny and spoke to me, in English. 'Lucky it was us that found you.'

I felt numb, frozen with horror. Johnny was dead, strung up by an angry mob. My mind refused to take it in. I stumbled along between the soldiers for what seemed like hours.

They took me to a guard-room at the top of a half-wrecked block of flats. As we climbed the creaking stairs I half-expected the whole building to crumble to the ground. A one-armed officer, his eyes red-rimmed from lack of sleep, asked me a few questions in German. When it became clear I couldn't understand him he gave a sigh and said something to a white-haired soldier, who took me back down the stairs again.

They kept me in a small room at the foot of the steps, close to the open door that led out to the street. I could have tried to escape, but where would I have gone? I was a prisoner in Berlin, the enemy capital, and a prisoner I would remain.

After a while, a girl arrived, riding a bike along the rubble-strewn road. I watched as she propped her bike against the wall outside. She seemed to be working as some kind of messenger. After delivering a note to the officer in the guard-room, she came back downstairs and sat down opposite me. I could see her eyeing my one bare foot, which was filthy and covered in dried blood. I'm sure the rest of me didn't look much better.

The girl was younger than I was, but not by much. Something about her reminded me of May Miller. I wondered if I'd ever see May again.

A lorry arrived and the white-haired soldier pointed to the door. It was time to go. As I left the room, the girl stood up and pushed something into my hand. It was a piece of bread.

I sat in the back of the truck and we drove through the shattered streets. We passed row upon row of ruined houses. There were bodies laid out on the pavements, their faces covered by blankets. Some of the dead were very small. Children.

In my hand was the crust of bread the girl had given me. I hadn't eaten for over 24 hours and I was ravenous. Nelson was dead. Johnny was dead. Hammers, Ron, Mitch and Dodge were all missing. But I was alive. That's all I knew.

A bird was perched in the blackened branches of a road-side tree. It was singing a shrill and joyous song, over and over. So it was spring-time here, too.

I thought about the girl in the guard-room. I'd come in a Lancaster bomber to destroy her city and to kill its people. Any one of the bombs from *M for Mother* might have killed her, or blown her arms and legs off, or trapped her under the rubble of her own home, with only the dead bodies of her family for company. But still she'd given me food. Tears rolled down my cheeks as I lifted the bread to my mouth and ate.